Nicholas
and the Gang

RENÉ GOSCINNY & JEAN-JACQUES SEMPÉ

Translated by Anthea Bell

Phaidon Press Limited
Regent's Wharf
All Saints Street
London N1 9PA

www.phaidon.com

This edition © 2007 Phaidon Press Limited
Reprinted in paperback 2011
First published in French as *Le petit Nicolas et les copains*
by Éditions Denoël © 1963 Éditions Denoël
New French edition © 2004 Éditions Denoël

ISBN 978 0 7148 6225 5
001-0611

A CIP catalogue record for this book is available
from the British Library.

Printed in China

CONTENTS

Matthew has Glasses

We were ever so surprised when Matthew arrived at school this morning, because he was wearing glasses. Matthew's all right; he's one of our gang. He's always bottom of the class, and it turns out that's why they gave him these glasses to wear.

'It was this doctor,' Matthew said. 'He told my mum and dad that maybe the reason I always came bottom was because I couldn't see the board too well in class. So they took me to the shop which sells glasses, and the man there looked at my eyes with a sort of thing which doesn't hurt, and he made me read lots of letters which didn't mean anything, and then he gave me glasses. So now I won't be bottom of the class any more!'

I was a bit surprised about the glasses, because the reason Matthew doesn't see things in class is that he's asleep a lot of the time, but perhaps these glasses will keep him awake. And it's a fact that Cuthbert, who's always top of the class, is the only other person who wears glasses, which is why we can't thump him as often as we'd like to.

Cuthbert wasn't too pleased to see Matthew wearing glasses. Cuthbert is teacher's pet, and he's always afraid someone else might come top of the class instead of him; so we were very pleased to know Matthew would be top of the class now, because Matthew's one of our gang and he's all right.

'Seen my glasses?' Matthew asked Cuthbert. 'I'm going to come top in everything now, and our teacher will be asking me to fetch the maps and wipe the board, so there!'

'Oh no, she won't! Oh no, she won't!' said Cuthbert. 'I'm top of the class, and anyway you don't have any right to come to school wearing glasses!'

'Oh, I don't, don't I?' said Matthew. 'Huh! You're not going to be the only soppy old teacher's pet now, so there!'

'I'm going to ask my dad to buy me some glasses,' said Rufus, 'and then I'll be top too!'

'We'll all ask our dads to buy us glasses!' shouted Geoffrey.

'Then we'll all be top of the class and we'll all be teacher's pet!'

And then it was great, because Cuthbert started shouting and crying, and he said it was a nasty mean trick, and we didn't have any right to be top of the class, and he was going to tell our teacher about us, and nobody loved him and he was very unhappy and he was going to kill himself, and then Old Spuds came chasing up. Old Spuds is one of our teachers, his real name is Mr Goodman, and some time I may tell you why we call him Old Spuds.

'What's going on here?' shouted Old Spuds. 'What's the matter with you, Cuthbert, carrying on like that? Now look me in the eye, boy, and tell me what's wrong!'

'They all want to wear glasses!' said Cuthbert, hiccupping like mad.

Old Spuds looked at Cuthbert, and then he looked at us, and he wiped his mouth with his hand, and then he said, 'Now then, all of you, look me in the eye! I don't intend to try and understand what you're going on about, all I say is that if I hear another squeak out of you I shall deal with you very severely! Cuthbert, go and hold your breath and drink a glass of water, and the rest of you just remember what I said!'

And he went off with Cuthbert, who was still hiccupping.

'Hey, can we borrow your glasses when the teacher asks us questions in class?' I asked Matthew.

'Yes, and when we're doing tests?'

'I'll need them myself when we're doing tests,' said Matthew, 'because if I don't come top my dad will know I wasn't wearing my glasses and then there'll be trouble. He doesn't like me to lend my things. But it's OK to borrow them for answering questions.'

Matthew really is all right! I asked him to let me have a go with his glasses, and honestly I don't see how Matthew's ever going to manage to come top, because when you put those glasses on everything looks all peculiar and your feet seem very close to your face. And then I passed the glasses on to Geoffrey, who lent them to Rufus, who handed them over to Jeremy, who gave them to Max, who threw them across to Eddie, and Eddie pretended to squint and he made us laugh a lot, and then Alec wanted a go, but we had a spot of trouble there.

'No, not you,' Matthew said. 'Your hands are covered in butter from your sandwiches and you'll get my glasses all dirty. I mean, it's not worth having glasses on if you can't see through them, and it's quite hard work cleaning them, and my dad won't let me watch television tonight if I come bottom again just because some silly twit got my glasses dirty with his great big buttery hands!'

And Matthew put his glasses back on, but Alec was annoyed.

'Want a smack in the face with my great big buttery hands?' Alec asked Matthew.

'You can't smack my face because I'm wearing glasses, so there!' said Matthew.

'Well, take them off, then,' said Alec.

'Shan't!' said Matthew.

'Huh!' Alec said. 'You're all the same when you get to be top of the class. Cowards, that's what you are!'

'I'm a coward?' shouted Matthew.

'Yes, because you're wearing glasses, so you're a coward!' shouted Alec.

'OK, we'll soon see who's a coward!' shouted Matthew, taking off his glasses.

They were both furious, but they didn't have time for much of a punch-up because Old Spuds came chasing up again.

'What is it now?' he asked.

'He doesn't want me to wear glasses!' shouted Alec.

'He wants to put butter all over mine!' shouted Matthew.

Old Spuds buried his face in his hands and then he drew his hands slowly down his cheeks, and when he does that it's not the best time to start acting up.

'Look me in the eye, boys! The pair of you!' said Old Spuds. 'I haven't the faintest notion what you've got into your heads this time, but I don't want to hear another word about glasses! And by tomorrow you will both write out a hundred times, "I must not say stupid things during break, thus causing trouble and forcing Mr Goodman, who is on duty, to intervene."'

And he went off to ring the bell for us to go into our classrooms.

While we were standing in line Matthew said he didn't mind lending Alec his glasses if Alec's hands were dry. Matthew's all right!

Next lesson was geography, and Matthew passed his glasses over to Alec, who had wiped his hands dry on his jacket. Alec put the glasses on, only he was out of luck because he didn't see our teacher standing right in front of him.

'Stop fooling about, Alec!' said our teacher. 'And don't squint! If the wind changed you might stay that way. Kindly leave the room!'

And Alec left the room, still wearing Matthew's glasses, and he nearly bumped into the door, and then our teacher told Matthew to come up to the blackboard and answer questions.

Matthew was quite right, it didn't work without the glasses. He got nought out of ten.

A Breath of Fresh Air

We'd been invited to spend Sunday at Mr Barlow's new country cottage. Mr Barlow is the accountant in the office where Dad works, and apparently he had a little boy of my own age, a very nice little boy called Conrad.

I was pleased, because I like going out into the country, and Dad told us Mr Barlow had bought his country cottage quite recently, and he'd told Dad it wasn't far from town. He gave Dad instructions for getting there over the telephone, and Dad wrote it all down on a piece of paper, and it was going to be dead easy! You just had to keep going straight on, turn left at the first traffic lights, go under the railway bridge, carry straight on again till you reached the crossroads, turn left, then left again, carry on till you came to a large white farmhouse, then turn right along a little country road, and then it was straight on and first left after the service station.

So Mum and Dad and I started off in the car quite early in the morning, and Dad was singing, and then he stopped singing because of all the other cars on the road. We were hardly moving at all. Then Dad missed the traffic lights where he was supposed to turn, but he said that didn't matter, he'd turn off and get back to the right road at the next crossroads. But there were lots of roadworks at the next crossroads, and they'd put up a notice saying 'Diversion', and we got lost. Dad shouted at Mum and told her she wasn't reading out the instructions on the piece of paper right, and Dad asked the way from no end of people who were strangers there themselves, and when we got to Mr Barlow's country cottage it was nearly lunchtime and we stopped arguing.

Mr Barlow came to meet us at the garden gate.

'Well, well, here come the city folks!' said Mr Barlow. 'Late risers back there in town, eh?'

So then Dad told him we'd been lost, and Mr Barlow looked very surprised.

'How on earth did you manage to get lost?' he said. 'Why, you only had to keep going straight ahead!'

And he took us into the cottage. Mr Barlow's cottage is fantastic! Not very big, but fantastic all the same!

'Wait a minute, and I'll call my wife,' said Mr Barlow. 'Claire! Claire! Our guests have arrived!' he shouted.

And Mrs Barlow came in. Her eyes were all red, and she was coughing, and she wore an apron covered in black smudges. 'I won't shake hands,' she told us, 'I'm covered in coal! I've been trying to get that stove to work since first thing this morning. No luck so far.'

Mr Barlow started to laugh.

'The fact is, we're a bit rustic out here,' he said. 'It's the wholesome country life, you see. We could hardly cook by electricity the way we do in our flat in town.'

'Why not?' asked Mrs Barlow.

'Well, well, we'll reconsider the situation in twenty years' time, when I've finished paying off the mortgage,' said Mr Barlow, and he started laughing again.

Mrs Barlow didn't do any laughing, and she went away saying, 'Please excuse me, I must see to the lunch. I think lunch may be a bit rustic too.'

'And how about young Conrad?' asked Dad. 'Isn't he here?'

'Oh, he's here all right!' said Mr Barlow. 'I sent the little so-and-so to his room to punish him. Know what he did when he got up this morning? I'll tell you: he climbed a tree to pick some plums! Do you realize, every one of those trees cost me a fortune, and I didn't buy them for that boy to amuse himself breaking branches, did I?'

Then Mr Barlow said well, since I was here he'd let Conrad out, because he was sure I was a good little boy who wouldn't go fooling about trampling all over the vegetable garden and the flower beds.

Conrad came down and he said hullo to Mum and Dad and he shook hands. Conrad looked OK. Not as OK as my gang at school, of course, but then you have to admit my gang at school are really great.

'Can we play in the garden?' I asked.

Conrad looked at his dad, and his dad said, 'I'd rather you didn't, boys. We'll be having lunch soon, and I don't want you bringing mud into the house. Mummy went to a lot of trouble cleaning the cottage this morning.'

So Conrad and I sat down, and while the grown-ups were

having a drink we looked at a magazine I'd already read at home. We read the magazine several times, because Mrs Barlow was late with the lunch. She wasn't having a drink with the other grown-ups. Then Mrs Barlow came in, taking off her apron, and she said, 'Well, too bad. It's lunchtime.'

Mr Barlow was very proud of the hors d'oeuvres we had to start with, because he told us the tomatoes had come from his own garden, and Dad laughed and said they seemed to have come rather early because they were still all green. Mr Barlow said maybe they weren't quite ripe yet, but the flavour was different from anything you could buy in a shop. What I liked best was the sardines.

And then Mrs Barlow brought in the joint, which was rather funny because it was all black outside, but inside it was just as if it hadn't been cooked at all.

'I don't want any,' said Conrad. 'I don't like raw meat.'

Mr Barlow frowned at him and told him to hurry up and finish his tomatoes and then eat up his meat like everyone else if he didn't want to be punished.

Something funny had happened to the roast potatoes round the joint too; they were rather hard inside.

After lunch we went and sat in the sitting room. Conrad read the magazine again, and Mrs Barlow told Mum how she had an au pair girl in town, but the au pair didn't like coming out into the country at weekends. Mr Barlow was telling

Dad how much the country cottage cost and what a bargain it was. I wasn't interested in any of that and so I asked Conrad if we could go outside and play, because the sun was shining. Conrad looked at his dad, and Mr Barlow said, 'Yes, of course, boys. Only mind you don't play on the lawns. Keep to the paths. Have a nice time and be good!'

Conrad and I went out. Conrad said we'd play boule; I'm dead good at boule. We played on the paths. Actually there was only one path and it wasn't very wide, and I have to admit Conrad played boule pretty well too.

'Watch out!' Conrad told me. 'If one of the boules goes on the lawn you can't have it back.'

And then Conrad aimed his boule and bonk! it hit mine and it went on the lawn and the window opened right away and Mr Barlow put his head out. He was all red in the face and he didn't look pleased.

'Conrad!' he shouted. 'How many times have I told you to be careful of that lawn? It's taken the gardener weeks to get it into decent condition! The moment you get out into the country you become quite impossible! Go up to your room and stay there till this evening.'

Conrad started to cry and he went upstairs, so I went back to the sitting room.

But we didn't stay very long, because Dad said he'd like to leave early so as to avoid the traffic jams. Mr Barlow said that was a good idea, and in fact they'd be starting back to town quite soon themselves, once Mrs Barlow had finished clearing up the cottage.

Mr and Mrs Barlow went out to the car with us. Dad and Mum told them it had been a day we'd never forget, and just as Dad was about to start Mr Barlow came up to the car door. 'Why don't you get a country cottage too?' Mr Barlow asked. 'Personally, of course, I hadn't set my heart on one, but one mustn't be selfish, old chap! You have no idea how much good it does my wife and son to relax and get out into the country for a breath of fresh air every Sunday!'

My Coloured Pencils

This morning the postman brought a parcel for me before I left for school. It was a present from Granny. That postman is great!

Dad was drinking his coffee, and he said, 'Oh lord, trouble ahead!' and Mum didn't like Dad saying that, and she started saying that whenever her mother, who is my granny, did anything, Dad found fault and Dad said he would really rather like to have his breakfast in peace, and Mum told him oh yes, she supposed she was only good enough to make breakfast and do the housework, right? Dad said he never said anything of the sort, but was it too much to ask for a little peace and quiet at home, when he had to work himself into the ground to provide the wherewithal for Mum to make breakfast anyway? And while Mum and Dad were talking I opened the parcel, and it was fantastic: it was a box of coloured pencils! I was so pleased I started running and jumping and dancing round the dining room with my box of pencils, and all the pencils fell out.

'Here we go again!' said Dad.

'I just don't understand your attitude!' said Mum. 'What's more, I don't see how anyone can cause any trouble with a box of coloured pencils, I really do not!'

'You soon will,' said Dad.

And he left for the office. Mum told me to pick up my coloured pencils because I was going to be late for school. So I put the pencils back in the box as fast as I could and I asked Mum if I could take them to school. Mum said yes, and she told me to mind not to cause any trouble with my coloured pencils and I promised not to. I put the box into my school bag and I left. Honestly, I can't make Mum and Dad out! Every time Granny sends me a present they're sure I'm going to do something silly with it!

I got to school just as the bell was ringing for us to go into our classrooms. I was very proud of my box of coloured pencils, and I couldn't wait to show it to our gang. The thing is, Geoffrey's the one who's always bringing presents his dad buys him to school, because his dad is very rich, and I was pleased I could show Geoffrey he wasn't the only one who got fantastic presents, was he, so there!

When lessons started our teacher asked Matthew to come up to the blackboard, and while she was asking him questions I showed my box to Alec, who was sitting beside me.

'Great!' said Alec.

'My granny sent them,' I told him.

'What's that?' asked Jeremy.

And Alec passed the box to Jeremy, who passed it to Rufus, who passed it to Geoffrey, who didn't look too pleased.

But they were all so busy opening the box and taking out the pencils to look at them, and trying them out, that I was afraid our teacher would notice, and then she might confiscate my pencils. So I started making signals to Geoffrey to give me back the box, and all of a sudden our teacher said, 'Nicholas, why are you fidgeting and making silly faces?'

That scared me, and I started crying, and I told her I had this box of coloured pencils my granny had sent me, and I wanted the others to give them back. Our teacher looked crossly at me, and then she sighed and she said, 'Very well. Will whoever has Nicholas's box kindly give it back?'

Geoffrey got up and he gave me back the box. And when I looked inside there were lots of pencils missing.

'What's the matter now?' our teacher asked me.

'Some of my pencils are missing,' I told her.

'Will anyone who has any of Nicholas's pencils kindly give them back?' said our teacher.

So then all my gang got up to come over and bring me back my pencils. Our teacher started tapping her desk with her ruler and she said we must all write out one hundred times:

'I must not use boxes of coloured pencils as an excuse to interrupt lessons and create chaos in the classroom.' The only one who didn't get any lines, apart from Cuthbert who is teacher's pet and he was away having mumps, was Matthew, who was answering questions up at the front of the class, and Matthew got kept in at break the same as every time he has to answer questions.

When the bell went for break I took my box of coloured pencils out with me so I could talk to my gang about them and not get any more lines. But when we were out in the playground and I opened the box the yellow pencil was still missing.

'I've lost my yellow pencil!' I shouted. 'Give me back my yellow pencil!'

'You and your pencils!' said Geoffrey. 'We're fed up with them! It's all your fault we got lines.'

So then I got very angry.

'It was because of you lot fooling around,' I said. 'I tell you what, you're all jealous, and if I don't find out who the thief is I'm going to tell our teacher on you!'

'It was Eddie who had the yellow pencil,' said Rufus, 'because he's red all over...hey, did you get that everyone? I made a joke: I said it was Eddie who pinched the yellow pencil because he was red all over!'

And they all started to laugh, and I laughed too because that was a good joke, and I thought I'd tell it to Dad. The only one who wasn't laughing was Eddie, who went up to Rufus and punched his nose.

'OK, so who stole the yellow pencil?

Say that again!' said Eddie, and he punched Geoffrey's nose.

'But I never said a word!' shouted Geoffrey, who doesn't like being punched on the nose, specially when it's Eddie doing the punching. That made me laugh, seeing Geoffrey punched on the nose when he wasn't expecting it! And Geoffrey came over to me and he thumped me when I wasn't expecting it, and I dropped my box of coloured pencils and we had a fight. Old Spuds, who was the teacher on duty, came running up and he parted us; he said we were a crowd of little savages; he said he hadn't the faintest wish to know what it was all about and he gave us all a hundred lines.

'I didn't have anything to do with it,' said Alec. 'I was eating my sandwich.'

'I didn't either,' said Jeremy, 'I was just asking Alec to give me a bit of his sandwich.'

'In your dreams!' said Alec.

So then Jeremy thumped Alec and Old Spuds gave them two hundred lines each.

When I got home at lunchtime I wasn't feeling happy; my box of coloured pencils was smashed and some of the pencils were broken and the yellow one was still missing. And when I got into the dining room I started crying and I told Mum about all the lines we had to do. Then Dad came in and he said, 'I see I was right to predict trouble ahead over those coloured pencils!'

'Oh, come, that's putting it rather strongly!' said Mum.

And then we heard a loud noise. It was Dad, falling over my yellow pencil, which was just outside the dining room door all the time, and he went and trod on it.

Going Camping

'Hey, you lot, how about going camping tomorrow?' Jeremy asked our gang when we were coming out of school.

'What's camping?' asked Matthew. Matthew's ever so funny, he never knows anything!

'Camping's great!' Jeremy told him. 'I went camping last weekend with my mum and dad and some friends of theirs. You go right out into the country by car, and then you find a good place beside a river and you put up tents and make a camp fire to cook lunch, and you bathe and you fish and you go to sleep in the tent, and there are midges and when it starts raining you all run for the car.'

'My mum and dad wouldn't let me go fooling about in the country on my own,' said Max. 'Specially not if there's a river.'

'No, I meant we'd play at going camping,' said Jeremy. 'Out on the bit of waste ground.'

'How about the tent, then?' asked Eddie. 'Got a tent, have you?'

'You bet!' said Jeremy. 'OK, everyone?'

So next day we went off to the bit of waste ground. I forget if I ever told you about that bit of waste ground: it's quite near my house and it's fantastic, all full of old crates and waste paper and stones, and empty tins and bottles and cats who get cross, and best of all there's this old car which hasn't got any wheels left, but it's great all the same.

Jeremy was last to arrive, with a folded blanket over his arm.

'Where's the tent?' asked Eddie.

'Well, here,' said Jeremy, showing us the blanket. It was an old blanket full of holes, with dirty marks all over it.

'That's not a proper tent!' said Rufus.

'You expect my dad to lend me his brand new tent?' said Jeremy. 'We can play that this blanket is a tent!'

So then Jeremy told us all to get in the car, because you have to go by car when you go camping.

'No, you don't!' said Geoffrey. 'My cousin's a Boy Scout, and when he goes camping he walks.'

'Well, if you want to walk, you just walk!' said Jeremy. 'But the rest of us are going by car and we'll arrive first, so there!'

'Who's the driver?' asked Geoffrey.

'Me, of course,' said Jeremy.

'Why you, then?' asked Geoffrey.

'Because going camping was my idea, and I brought the tent,' said Jeremy.

Geoffrey wasn't too pleased, but we wanted to get there quick and start camping, so we made him shut up. Then we all got in the car, and we put the tent on the roof, and we all went 'vroom vroom' except for Jeremy who was driving, and he was yelling, 'Watch out, Grandpa! Move over, roadhog! Menace to

the public! Hey, did you see me overtake that sports car?'
Jeremy's going to be a marvellous driver when he grows up!
Then he said, 'This looks like a good place. Let's stop here.'

So we all stopped going 'vroom vroom' and we got out of
the car. Jeremy looked round with a big grin on his face.

'This'll do fine! Fetch the tent, the river isn't far away.'

'I don't see any river,' said Rufus. 'Where's the river?'

'Over there, of course!' said Jeremy. 'We're playing at
camping, aren't we?'

So we got the tent off the car roof, and while we were
putting it up Jeremy told Geoffrey and Matthew to go and get
water from the river and then play at lighting a fire to cook
lunch.

It wasn't too easy, putting up that tent, but we stood some
crates on top of each other and spread the blanket over them
and it was great.

'Lunch is ready!' shouted Geoffrey.

So then we all played at eating, except for Alec who was
really eating, because he'd brought some jam sandwiches
from home.

'This is lovely chicken!' said Jeremy. 'Yum yum!'

'Pass the jam sandwiches, will you?' Max asked Alec.

'Are you nuts?' said Alec. 'I didn't ask you to pass the
chicken, did I?'

But Alec's our friend, he's OK, so he played at passing Max
one of his jam sandwiches.

'Right, now we have to put out the fire and bury all the
litter,' said Jeremy.

'You must be off your head!' said Rufus. 'If you want us to
bury all the litter on the waste ground we'll be here for days!'

'How thick can you get?' said Jeremy. 'We just play at burying the litter! Now we all lie down inside the tent and go to sleep.'

That was fantastic. We were all squashed up inside the tent, and it was ever so hot, but we had a great time. Of course we didn't really go to sleep because we weren't sleepy, and there wasn't room either. We'd been lying down inside the tent for a moment when Alec said, 'Now what do we do?'

'Well, nothing special,' said Jeremy. 'Anyone who wants can have a rest, and the others go and bathe in the river. That's the great thing about camping, you can do whatever you want.'

'If I'd brought my Indian headdress we could have played Indians in this tent,' said Eddie.

'Play Indians?' said Jeremy. 'Ever seen any Indians out camping, you soppy great nit?'

'Who's a soppy great nit?' asked Eddie.

'Eddie's right,' said Rufus. 'It's boring, having a rest in this silly old tent!'

'You're a soppy great nit!' said Jeremy, which wasn't very sensible, because you can't go fooling around with Eddie. Eddie's very strong, and he punched Jeremy's nose, bonk! And Jeremy got annoyed, so he started fighting Eddie. There wasn't too much room in the tent, and we were all getting thumped, and then the crates fell over and we had a bit of trouble getting out from underneath the tent, and it was fantastic! But Jeremy wasn't too pleased, and he kicked the blanket and he shouted, 'Well, if you don't like my tent you can just get out of it and I'll go camping on my own, so there!'

'Are you really annoyed or are you playing at being annoyed?' asked Rufus.

So then we all laughed a lot and Rufus laughed too, and he asked, 'Hey, what did I say that was so funny? Come on, what did I say that was so funny?'

And then Alec said it was getting late and he had to go home for supper.

'That's right,' said Jeremy, 'and anyway, it's raining! Come on, quick! Pick up all the stuff and run for the car!'

Going camping was terrific, and by the time we got home we were all tired but happy, even if our mums and dads did tell us off for being late.

And that wasn't fair, because we couldn't help it if the car got stuck in a huge big traffic jam on the way back, could we?

Talking on the Radio

This morning at school our teacher told us, 'Boys, I have an exciting piece of news for you! Some reporters from the radio are coming to interview you in the context of a big survey being conducted among schoolchildren.'

We didn't say anything because we didn't know what she meant, except for Cuthbert, but it wasn't specially clever of him to know because he's teacher's pet and top of the class. So then our teacher explained that some gentlemen from the radio would be coming to ask us questions. They were doing that in all the schools in town, and it was our school's turn today.

'And I'm counting on you all to behave well and give intelligent replies,' said our teacher.

We were ever so excited to think we were going to be on the radio, and our teacher had to bang her desk with her ruler several times before we could go on learning any grammar.

Then the classroom door opened and the Head came in with two men. One of them was carrying a suitcase.

'Stand up, boys!' said our teacher.

'Sit down, boys!' said the Head. 'Now, boys, it is a great honour for our school to go on air! Thanks to the genius of Marconi, the magic of radio waves will carry your words to thousands of households! I'm sure you appreciate this honour, and that you feel a true sense of responsibility. And I warn you that anyone who lets his imagination run away with him will be punished severely! Now, this gentleman will explain what he wants you to do.'

So then one of the men told us he was going to ask us questions about our hobbies and the books we read and the stuff we learnt at school. And then he picked something up and said, 'This is a microphone. You speak into it, clearly and distinctly, and don't sound nervous! It's all being recorded, so you'll be able to hear yourselves on the air at eight o'clock this evening.'

Then he looked at the other man, who had opened his case, and put it on our teacher's desk, and there were machines and things in the case, and he'd put some things over his ears to listen through. Like the pilots in a film I saw, only their radio wasn't working and it was very foggy so they couldn't find the town where they were supposed to land and they crashed into the sea, and it was a really fantastic film! And the first man said to the one with the things on his ears, 'Ready to go, Pete?'

'Right,' said Mr Pete. 'Test for voice level, will you?'

'One, two, three, four, five. OK?' asked the other man.

'OK, Jim,' said Mr Pete.

'Right,' said Mr Jim. 'Well, who'd like first go?'

'Me! Me! Me!' we all shouted.

Mr Jim started laughing and he said, 'I see we have plenty of volunteers! I think I'd better ask your teacher here to pick someone.'

And of course our teacher told them to ask Cuthbert questions, because he's top of the class and teacher's pet so he always does get asked questions. Honestly, I ask you!

So Cuthbert went up to Mr Jim, and Mr Jim held the microphone in front of Cuthbert's face, and Cuthbert's face went all white.

'Well now, what's your name?' asked Mr Jim.

Cuthbert opened his mouth and nothing came out. So then Mr Jim said, 'You're Cuthbert, aren't you?'

Cuthbert nodded.

'And I hear you're top of the class,' said Mr Jim. 'Now, what we'd like to know is what you do in your spare time, what games you like to play...come along, speak up! There's nothing to be afraid of!'

So then Cuthbert started to cry, and then he felt sick, and our teacher had to take him out of the room in a hurry.

Mr Jim wiped his forehead, and he looked at Mr Pete, and then he asked, 'Is there anyone here who isn't scared of microphones?'

'Me! Me! Me!' we all shouted.

'Right,' said Mr Jim. 'You, come here...yes, the fat little boy. That's it. Right, off we go. Well now, what's your name?'

'It's Alec,' said Alec.

'Ishalec?' asked Mr Jim, surprised.

'Please be good enough not to speak with your mouth full!' said the Head.

'Well, I just happened to be eating my croissant, didn't I?' said Alec.

'You...you mean you boys eat during lessons these days?' shouted the Head. 'I must say! Go and stand in the corner, Alec. We will sort this out later, and meanwhile leave that croissant on your teacher's desk.'

So Alec sighed, deeply, left his croissant on our teacher's desk and went to stand in the corner, where he started eating the brioche he'd taken out of his trouser pocket. Mr Jim was wiping the microphone on his sleeve.

'Please forgive them!' said the Head. 'They're very young, you know, and a little unruly.'

'Oh, we're used to that kind of thing,' said Mr Jim, laughing. 'We interviewed the striking dockers on our last assignment, didn't we, Pete?'

'Those were the days,' said Mr Pete.

Then Mr Jim picked out Eddie.

'Well now, what's your name?' he asked.

'Eddie!' shouted Eddie, and Mr Pete took off the thing he had on his ears.

'Not so loud!' said Mr Jim. 'That's why they invented radio, you know, so people could hear each other a long way off, without shouting! Let's try again...well now, what's your name?'

'Eddie, of course. I've told you already!' said Eddie.

'No, no!' said Mr Jim. 'You don't want to tell me you've told me already! I ask your name and then you tell me, that's all. Ready, Pete? OK, we'll start again...well now, what's your name?'

'Eddie,' said Eddie.

'Never!' said Geoffrey.

'Geoffrey, leave the room!' said the Head.

'Shut up, all of you!' shouted Mr Jim.

'For heaven's sake, give me advance warning when you're about to do that!' said Mr Pete, taking the things off his ears again. Mr Jim covered his eyes with his hand for a moment, then he took his hand away again and he asked Eddie what he liked doing in his spare time.

'Playing football,' said Eddie. 'I'm fantastic at football! I'm the greatest!'

'Liar!' I said. 'You were in goal yesterday, and who let the ball get past him into the net, then?'

'You did, right, Eddie?' said Matthew.

'Rufus had whistled for offside!' said Eddie.

'You bet he had!' said Max. 'He was playing for your team, and if you ask me I still don't think one of the players can be referee too, even if he is the only person with a whistle.'

'Want me to punch your nose?' asked Eddie, and the Head gave him detention. Then Mr Jim said it was all in the can, Mr Pete put all his things back in the case, and they both went away.

So at eight o'clock at home this evening we were sitting round the radio, me and Mum and

Dad, and Mr and Mrs Billings and Mr and Mrs Campbell, who live next door, and Mr Collins who works in the same office as my dad, and Uncle George, and we were to hear me on the radio. Granny had been told too late for her to come, but she was listening at home and she'd invited some friends in. Dad was very proud, and he kept patting my head and chuckling, and everyone was looking very pleased.

But something must have gone wrong with the radio programme, because when eight o'clock came they only broadcast some music.

The people I really feel sorry for are Mr Jim and Mr Pete. They must have been so disappointed!

Mary Jane

Mum said I could invite the gang from school to tea, and I asked Mary Jane too. Mary Jane has yellow hair and blue eyes and she's the daughter of Mr and Mrs Campbell who live in the house next door.

When the gang arrived Alec went straight off to the dining room to see what there was for tea, and when he came back he asked, 'Is someone else coming? I counted the chairs, and there's going to be one piece of cake left over.' So I told him I'd invited Mary Jane, and I explained about her being the daughter of Mr and Mrs Campbell who live next door.

'But she's a girl!' said Geoffrey.

'Well, yes,' I said. 'So what?'

'We don't play with any soppy old girls!' said Matthew. 'If she comes we shan't talk to her and we shan't play with her, so there!'

'I'll invite anyone I like to tea,' I said, 'and if you don't like that then I'll thump you.'

But I didn't have time to thump him, because the doorbell rang and Mary Jane came in.

She was wearing a dress made of that velvety kind of stuff like the big curtains in the sitting room, only dark green, with a white collar which had lots of little holes around the edge.

Mary Jane looked terrific! The only trouble was, she'd brought a doll with her.

'Well, Nicholas, aren't you going to introduce Mary Jane to the boys?' asked Mum.

'This one's Eddie,' I said, 'and that's Rufus and Matthew and Geoffrey and Alec.'

'And this is my dolly,' said Mary Jane. 'She's called Cindy, and her dress is made of real silk.'

Since none of us could think of anything to say, Mum said we might as well go into the dining room and have tea.

Mary Jane sat between me and Alec. Mum gave us hot chocolate to drink, and handed round the slices of cake, and it was very nice, but still no one said anything. We might as well have been at school when the inspector's due to come round. Then Mary Jane looked at Alec and she said to him, 'Don't you eat fast! I never saw anyone eat as fast as you! It's fantastic!'

And she batted her eyelashes very fast, several times.

Alec didn't bat an eyelash at all; he just gawped at Mary Jane; he swallowed the big piece of cake he had in his mouth, went bright red, and gave a silly sort of laugh.

'Huh!' said Geoffrey. 'I can eat as fast as him! I can eat even faster if I want to!'

'You must be joking!' said Alec.

'Oh no!' said Mary Jane. 'I don't see how anyone *could* eat faster than Alec.'

And Alec gave his silly laugh again. So then Geoffrey said, 'OK, we'll see.'

And he started eating the rest of his cake as fast as he possibly could. Alec couldn't join in the race because he'd already finished his slice, but the others tried racing Geoffrey.

'I've won!' shouted Eddie, spraying crumbs all over the place.

'That doesn't count,' said Rufus. 'You hardly had any cake left anyway.'

'I did!' said Eddie. 'I'd only just started it!'

'Don't make me laugh!' said Matthew. 'Mine was the biggest piece, so I've won.'

I wanted to thump Matthew again, for cheating this time, but Mum came in, and when she looked at the table she was very surprised.

'Goodness me!' she said. 'Have you finished that cake already?'

'I haven't finished my piece yet,' said Mary Jane. Mary Jane takes small mouthfuls, and takes ages to finish, because before she puts any cake in her mouth she keeps offering her doll a bite, but of course the doll doesn't eat it.

'Very well,' said Mum. 'When you've finished, you can go and play in the garden. It's a nice fine day.'

And she went out.

'Got your football?' Matthew asked me.

'Good idea!' said Rufus. 'You lot may be world class cake-eating champions, but I'm the best at football! I can get the ball past anyone!'

'Don't make me laugh!' said Geoffrey.

'I'll tell you who's ever so good at turning somersaults,' said Mary Jane. 'Nicholas is.'

'Somersaults?' said Eddie. 'I'm the best at somersaults! I've been turning somersaults for years.'

'You've got a nerve!' I said. 'You know perfectly well I'm the greatest at somersaults!'

'Want to bet?' said Eddie.

And we all went out into the garden, including Mary Jane, who had finished her cake at last, for me and Eddie to have a somersault competition.

We started turning somersaults right away, and then Geoffrey said well, he didn't know, and he turned somersaults too. Rufus isn't all that good at somersaults, and Matthew had to stop almost at once because he had a marble in his pocket and he lost it in the grass. Mary Jane watched and clapped us, and Alec stood beside her, with a brioche he'd brought from home to eat after tea in one hand and Mary Jane's doll Cindy in the other. What really surprised me was to see Alec offering bits of his brioche to the doll, because usually he won't give anyone anything to eat, not even our gang!

Matthew, who'd found his marble, said, 'Well, can you do this?' And he started walking on his hands.

'Ooh!' said Mary Jane. 'Aren't you clever?'

Walking on your hands is harder than turning somersaults; I tried it, but I kept falling over. Eddie was pretty good at it, and he managed to stay up there on his hands longer than Matthew, but perhaps that was because Matthew's marble had fallen out of his pocket again and he had to start looking for it for the second time.

'What's the point of walking on your hands, anyway?' said Rufus. 'Now, climbing trees is useful!'

44

And Rufus started climbing our tree, and I have to admit the tree in our garden isn't all that easy to climb, because it hasn't got many branches, and they're all high up near the leaves at the top.

So we all stood there laughing at Rufus, who was clinging to the tree with his hands and feet, but not getting along very fast.

'Shove off!' said Geoffrey. 'I'll show you!'

But Rufus didn't want to let go of the tree, and then Geoffrey and Matthew both tried climbing it at once, with Rufus shouting, 'Look at me! Look at me! I'm climbing!'

It was a bit of luck Dad wasn't there, because he isn't too keen on people fooling around with our tree. Eddie was turning somersaults again and so was I, because there wasn't any room left for us on the tree, and Mary Jane was counting to see which of us turned most.

And then Mrs Campbell called across from her own garden, 'Come along in, Mary Jane! Time for your piano lesson!'

So Mary Jane got her doll back from Alec, and she waved goodbye to us and went home.

Rufus, Geoffrey and Matthew came down from the tree, Eddie stopped turning somersaults, and Alec said, 'It's late. I'd better be going.'

It was a great tea party, and we had a lot of fun, but I'm not too sure if Mary Jane enjoyed herself.

The thing is, I'm afraid we weren't really very nice to Mary Jane. We hardly said anything to her at all, we just went on playing as if she hadn't been there!

Collecting Stamps

Rufus looked ever so pleased with himself when he got to school this morning. He showed us a brand new exercise book with a stamp stuck on the top left hand corner of the first page. There wasn't anything at all on the other pages.

'I'm starting a stamp collection,' Rufus told us.

And he explained it was his dad who'd given him the idea of collecting stamps, which was really called philately, and it was terribly useful too, because you could learn a lot of history and geography from looking at the stamps. His dad had told him that a stamp collection could be worth a great deal of money, and some old King of England had a collection which was very valuable indeed.

'The best idea,' Rufus told us, 'would be if all the rest of you collected stamps too, and then we could swap. Dad told me that's the way to get a really good collection. But the stamps mustn't be torn, and they have to have all their perforated dog-tooth edges showing.'

When I got home at lunchtime I asked Mum for some stamps.

'What's all this about?' asked Mum. 'Go and wash your hands, do, and don't bother me with your silly notions!'

'Why do you want stamps, Nicholas?' Dad asked me. 'Are you going to write some letters?'

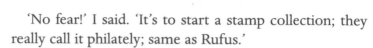

'No fear!' I said. 'It's to start a stamp collection; they really call it philately; same as Rufus.'

'I call that a good idea!' said Dad. 'Philately is a very interesting hobby! You can learn a lot from collecting stamps, especially history and geography. And a really good collection can be very valuable, you know. King George V of England had one which was worth a fortune!'

'Yes,' I said, 'and I can swap stamps with the gang and we'll have fantastic collections with no end of dogs' teeth in the stamps!'

'Er...yes,' said Dad. 'Well, anyway, I'd rather see you collect stamps than those useless toys which clutter up your pockets and the whole house. Now, do as your mother says, go and wash your hands, then we'll have lunch, and after lunch I'll give you some stamps!'

So after lunch Dad looked in his desk, and he found three envelopes and tore off the corners with the stamps on them.

'There you are! The start of a remarkable collection!' said Dad, laughing.

And I hugged him, because my dad is the best dad in the whole world.

When I got back to school that afternoon lots of the gang had started collecting stamps; Matthew had one stamp, Geoffrey had another stamp, and Alec had a stamp too, but it was all torn and buttery and lots of its edges were missing. Mine was the best collection, because I had three stamps. Eddie didn't have any at all, and he told us we were nuts, stamp collecting was no use, he'd rather play football.

'You're the one who's nuts,' said Rufus. 'If that old King George had played football instead of collecting stamps he wouldn't have got so rich! Maybe he wouldn't even have been king!'

Rufus was right, but the bell rang for lessons just then, so we couldn't go on with our stamp collecting. At break we all started swapping.

'Who wants my stamp?' asked Alec.

'You've got a stamp I haven't got,' Rufus told Matthew. 'Want to swap?'

'OK,' said Matthew. 'I'll swap you my stamp for two other stamps.'

'So why should I give you two stamps for one stamp?' asked Rufus. 'I'll swap you one stamp for one stamp!'

'I don't mind swapping my one stamp for one stamp,' said Alec.

And then Old Spuds came over. Old Spuds was on playground duty, and he gets suspicious when he sees our gang all together, and since our gang is always together because our gang is a fantastic gang, Old Spuds is suspicious all the time.

'Look me in the eye, boys!' said Old Spuds. 'Now, what are you lot up to this time?'

'Nothing, sir,' said Matthew. 'We're collecting stamps and then we're swapping them. One stamp for two stamps, and so on, and that way we'll build up valuable collections.'

'Stamp collecting?' said Old Spuds. 'I call that a good idea! Very good! Most educational, especially when it comes to history and geography. And stamp collections can sometimes be very valuable. There was this king…well, I forget his name and where he was king of, but he had a collection which was worth a fortune, anyway! Very well, you may go on swapping, but behave yourselves!'

49

So Old Spuds went away and Matthew offered his stamp to Rufus.

'Is it a deal?' asked Matthew.

'No,' said Rufus.

'I'll do a deal with you,' said Alec.

And then Eddie came up to Matthew and he took Matthew's stamp away from him.

'I'm starting a collection too!' said Eddie, laughing like a drain. Then he started to run. Matthew, who wasn't laughing at all, ran after Eddie shouting that he was a dirty thief and he was to give him back his stamp. So then Eddie, still running, licked the stamp and stuck it on his own forehead.

'Hey, look, everyone!' shouted Eddie. 'Look at me! I'm a letter! I'm an airmail letter!'

And Eddie spread his arms out and started running round going 'vroom, vroom,' like a plane, but Matthew managed to trip him up, and Eddie fell over, and they started having a really great punch-up, and Old Spuds came chasing up again.

'I might have known I couldn't trust you!' said Old Spuds.

'You're quite unable to amuse yourselves intelligently! You two, go and stand in the corner! As for you, Eddie, kindly take that ridiculous stamp off your forehead!'

'Tell him to be careful not to tear the edges,' said Rufus. 'It's one of the stamps I haven't got.'

And Old Spuds sent him to stand in the corner with Matthew and Eddie.

So now the only stamp collectors left were Geoffrey and Alec and me.

'Listen, you lot, don't you want my stamp?' asked Alec.

'I'll swap your three stamps for my stamp,' said Geoffrey to me.

'Are you nuts?' I asked Geoffrey. 'If you want my three stamps you'll have to give me three other stamps, so there! I'll give you a stamp for a stamp.'

'I don't mind giving you a stamp for a stamp,' said Alec.

'Well, what good would that do me?' Geoffrey asked me. 'Your stamps are the same as my stamp!'

'So nobody wants my stamp?' asked Alec.

'OK, I'll swap you my three stamps for something else. Something really good,' I told Geoffrey.

'Right,' said Geoffrey.

'Well, if nobody wants my stamp, too bad!' said Alec, and he tore up his stamp collection.

When I got home I was feeling very pleased with myself, and Dad asked me, 'Well, young philatelist, how's the stamp collection coming along?'

'It's great!' I told him.

And I showed him the two marbles Geoffrey had given me.

Max's Conjuring Tricks

Our gang was invited to tea at Max's house which was surprising, because Max never invites anyone home, his mum doesn't like him to. But he told us his uncle, the one who's a sailor but I don't think that's true, I don't believe he's a sailor at all, well, anyway this uncle had given him a box of magic tricks, and doing conjuring tricks isn't any fun without an audience, so that was why Max's mum said he could ask us to tea.

When I arrived the rest of the gang were already there, and Max's mum gave us tea; it wasn't anything special, bread and butter, and tea to drink, and we were all looking at Alec, who was eating some little chocolate croissants he'd brought from home, but it's no use asking Alec for any of his chocolate croissants, because Alec's all right, he's one of our gang, and he'll lend you anything you like but not something to eat.

After tea Max took us into the sitting room. He'd put chairs in rows, like at Matthew's house when Matthew's dad put on a silly show for us, and Max stood behind a table with the box of magic tricks on it. Max opened the box; it was full of all sorts of things, and he took out a wand and a big dice.

'You see this dice?' asked Max. 'It's extra big, but apart from that it's the same as any other dice…'

'No, it isn't,' said Geoffrey. 'It's hollow, and there's another dice inside.'

Max's jaw dropped and he looked at Geoffrey.

'How do you know?' asked Max.

'I know because I've got the same box of magic tricks at home,' said Geoffrey. 'My dad gave it to me when I came twelfth in the spelling test.'

'You mean there's a catch in it?' asked Rufus.

'No, there's not a catch in it!' shouted Max. 'Geoffrey's a dirty liar, that's what!'

'I tell you that dice is hollow,' said Geoffrey, 'and if you want to be thumped just call me a dirty liar again!'

But they never got round to fighting properly, because Max's mum came into the sitting room. She looked at us, and she stood still for a moment, and then she went away, sighing, and carrying a lamp which had been standing on the mantelpiece. I was interested in this hollow dice, and so I went up to the table to have a look at it.

'No!' shouted Max. 'No! Go back to your seat, Nicholas! You're not allowed to come close!'

'Why not?' I asked.

'Because there's a catch in it, you bet!' said Rufus.

'That's right,' said Geoffrey. 'The dice is hollow, see? So when you put it down on the table, the other dice inside it...'

'If you carry on like that you can just go home!' shouted Max.

And Max's mum came into the sitting room, and she went out again with a little statue which was standing on the piano.

Then Max put the dice away and he picked up a kind of small saucepan.

'This saucepan is empty,' Max said, showing it to us.

And he looked at Geoffrey, but Geoffrey was busy explaining the trick with the hollow dice to Matthew, who hadn't understood it.

'I know!' said Jeremy. 'The saucepan's empty, and you're going to take a white pigeon out of it.'

'If he does, there's a catch in it,' said Rufus.

'Pigeon?' said Max. 'Don't be daft! Where do you suppose I'd get a white pigeon, you silly twit?'

'I saw a conjuror on the telly and he was taking lots of pigeons out of everywhere, so silly twit yourself!' said Jeremy.

'Anyway,' said Max, 'even if I wanted to take pigeons out of the saucepan I couldn't, because my mum doesn't like me having animals in the house, and there was trouble that time I brought a mouse home, and who were you calling a silly twit, then?'

'That's a pity,' said Alec. 'I like pigeons. They're rather small, but if you stuff them and then stew them they taste lovely, like chicken!'

'You're a silly twit,' Jeremy told Max, 'that's who's a silly twit!'

And Max's mum came in, and I'm not too sure she wasn't listening at the door, and she told us to be good boys and mind not to touch the lamp in the corner.

When she went out again Max's mum was looking rather worried...

'That saucepan,' said Matthew. 'Is that hollow too, like the dice?'

'Not exactly,' said Geoffrey, 'it's got a false bottom.'

'I knew there was a catch in it!' said Rufus.

Then Max got angry, and he told us we were a rotten lot of friends, and he closed his box of magic tricks and said he wasn't going to do any more of them. And he started to sulk, and no one said anything. And then Max's mum came chasing in, full tilt.

'Whatever's going on
in here?' she shouted. 'I
can't hear anything!'

'It's them!' said Max.
'They won't let me do my
magic tricks!'

'Listen, children,' said
Max's mum. 'I'm very pleased
to see you having a nice time,
but you must behave or you'll have
to go home! I've just got to pop out and do
some shopping, but I know you'll be big, sensible
boys, and whatever you do don't touch the clock on
the cupboard.'

And Max's mum took another look at us, and she went out,
shaking her head and looking up at the ceiling.

'Right,' said Max. 'See this white ball? Well, I'm going to
make it disappear.'

'Is there a catch in it?' asked Rufus.

'Yes,' said Geoffrey, 'he's going to hide it and put it in his
pocket.'

'Oh no, I'm not!' shouted Max. 'Oh no, I'm not! I really and
truly am going to make it disappear, so there!'

'No, you aren't,' said Geoffrey. 'I know what you're going to
do, you're going to put it in your pocket, you're not going to
make it disappear!'

'Well, can he make that white ball disappear or can't he?'
asked Eddie.

'Of course I could make it disappear if I wanted to!' said
Max. 'But I don't want to, because you're being so mean, so

57

that's your bad luck! My mum was right to say you were a set of young hooligans!'

'There, what did I tell you?' said Geoffrey. 'It'd take a real conjuror to make that ball disappear, not a stupid amateur like him!'

So then Max got angry and he made for Geoffrey and thumped him, and Geoffrey didn't like that, so he threw the box of magic tricks on the floor and he got angry too, and he and Max started a tremendous punch-up. We were having a great time, and then Max's mum came into the sitting room, and she didn't look at all pleased.

'Go home, all of you!' Max's mum told us. 'Go home this minute!'

So we went home, and I was rather disappointed, even though it had been a fantastic afternoon, because I'd have liked to see Max do his magic tricks.

'Huh!' said Matthew. 'I think Rufus is right. Max isn't like the real conjurors on the telly. Everything he does is just a trick!'

And next day at school Max was still furious with us, because it turned out that when he picked up his box of magic tricks, he'd found out that the white ball had disappeared.

A Rainy Day

I like it when it rains really hard, because then I don't go to school and I can stay at home instead and play with my electric train set. But today it wasn't raining quite hard enough for that, so I had to go to school.

Actually it's quite fun going to school in the rain; you can put your head back and open your mouth to catch the raindrops, and you can walk in puddles and splash water all over your friends, you can walk under leaking gutters and it's ever so cold when the water trickles down your neck inside your shirt, because of course walking under gutters with your raincoat buttoned right up doesn't count. The only trouble is, when break comes they won't let us out into the playground in case we get wet.

We had the light on in our classroom, and that made everything look funny; one thing I like doing is watching the raindrops race each other down the window panes. They look like rivers. And then the bell went, and our teacher told us, 'Well, it's break now. You can talk to each other, but mind you're good.'

So then we all started talking at once, and there was an awful lot of noise; you really had to shout to make yourself heard, and our teacher sighed; she stood up and she went out into the corridor leaving the door open, to go and talk to the other teachers, who aren't as nice as our teacher, who really is very nice so we try not to annoy her too much.

'Come on,' said Eddie. 'How about a game of dodge ball?'

'Are you nuts?' asked Rufus. 'Our teacher won't like it, and you know we're bound to break a window pane.'

'Well then, all we have to do is open the window!' said Jeremy.

That was a great idea, and we all went over to the window, except for Cuthbert who was revising history by reading his history book out loud with his hands over his ears. Cuthbert is nuts! And then we opened the window; it was great because the wind was blowing towards our classroom and we had fun getting water in our faces, and then we heard a screech, and it was our teacher coming back in.

'You must be crazy!' our teacher shouted. 'Kindly close that window this minute!'

'It was so we could play dodge ball,' Jeremy explained.

So then our teacher told us we were not to play dodge ball and that was that; she made us close the window and she told us all to sit down. The trouble was, the desks near the window were all wet now, and it's fun getting rain on your face but it isn't any fun sitting in it. Our teacher waved her arms about in the air and she said we were hopeless, and we'd better squeeze into the dry desks. So that meant quite a bit of noise, because everyone was looking for a place to sit down, and there were some desks with five people in them, and it's quite a squash fitting more than three at a time into the desks. I was sharing

a desk with Rufus and Matthew and Eddie. And then our teacher banged her own desk with her ruler and she shouted, 'Silence!' And no one said anything except for Cuthbert, who hadn't heard her, and he was reciting history dates out loud. Actually he was at a desk all on his own, because no one ever wants to sit next to teacher's pet except in tests. Then Cuthbert looked up and he saw our teacher's face and he stopped talking.

'Right!' said our teacher. 'The first boy to do anything will regret it, understand? I don't want another squeak out of you! Now, try and sort yourselves out rather better in the dry desks, and do it in silence.'

So we all got up, and we changed places without saying anything. It wasn't a good moment to act up, because our teacher really did look very cross. I was sitting with Geoffrey, Max, Matthew and Alec now, and we weren't very comfortable because Alec takes up an awful lot of space and his sandwiches leave crumbs everywhere. Our teacher looked at us for a bit, and then she sighed, and then she went out again to talk to the other teachers.

Then Geoffrey got up and went over to the blackboard, and he picked up the chalk and drew ever such a funny man, even if the man didn't have a nose, and he wrote 'Max is a halfwit' under the picture. That made us all laugh, except for Cuthbert who had gone back to reciting dates and Max who went over to Geoffrey to thump him. Of course Geoffrey started thumping him back, but honestly we'd hardly started shouting at all when our teacher came back in a hurry, very red in the face and looking very cross; I hadn't seen her look as cross as that for at least a week. When she saw the blackboard it was worse than ever.

'Who did that?' asked our teacher.

'Geoffrey,' said Cuthbert.

'Dirty sneak!' said Geoffrey. 'I'm going to thump you, you see if I don't!'

'That's right! Go on, Geoffrey!' shouted Max.

After that it was great. Our teacher was ever so angry, and she kept on banging her desk with her ruler, and Cuthbert started shouting and crying and saying no one loved him and it wasn't fair and everyone took advantage of him, and he was going to die and he'd tell his parents on us, and we were all running about and shouting and having a fantastic time.

'Sit down!' shouted our teacher.

'For the last time, sit down! I don't want another word out of you! Sit down!'

So we sat down. I was sitting in a desk with Rufus, Max and Jeremy, and the Head came into our classroom.

'Stand up, boys!' said our teacher.

'Sit down, boys!' said the Head.

Then he looked at us, and he asked our teacher, 'What on earth is going on in here? We can hear the noise your class is making all over the school! And why are they sitting four or five to a desk when some of the desks are empty? All of you get back to your places!'

We all stood up, but our teacher told the Head about the wet desks. The Head looked surprised but he said all right, we could go back to the desks we'd just left. So now I was sharing a desk with Alec, Rufus, Matthew, Jeremy and Eddie, and it was a bit crowded. Then the Head pointed to the blackboard and he asked, 'Who drew that? Come along, own up!'

And Cuthbert didn't have to tell him, because Geoffrey got up, crying and saying it wasn't his fault.

'It's rather late in the day for tears, young man,' said the Head. 'I can see you've started down the slippery slope that leads I hate to think where, but I intend to cure you of the habit of using vulgar language to insult your friends. You will copy out the sentence you wrote on the blackboard five hundred times, understand? As for the rest of you, even though it has stopped raining you will not go into the playground at all today! You will stay in your classroom under your teacher's supervision, to teach you the value of disciplined behaviour!'

And when the Head had gone out and we'd sat down at our

desk again, along with Geoffrey and Max, we realized how nice our teacher is, and how much she likes us even though we sometimes make her angry. Because she looked even more annoyed than we did when she heard we weren't going to be allowed out into the playground today!

Playing Chess

On Sunday it was cold and wet, but I didn't mind that, because I'd been invited to tea at Alec's house, and Alec is a friend of mine; he's all right. He's very fat and he loves eating, and I always have a great time with Alec, even when we're arguing.

When I got to Alec's house it was his mum who opened the door, because Alec and his dad had already sat down to their tea and they were only waiting for me to start.

'You're late,' said Alec.

'Don't talk with your mouth full, and pass the butter,' said his dad.

We each had two big cups of hot chocolate to drink, a cream cake, hot buttered toast and jam, salami, cheese, and when we'd finished Alec asked his mum if we could have some of the chicken casserole left over from lunch, because he'd like me to have a taste of it, but his mum said no, it would spoil our appetites for supper, and anyway there wasn't any of the chicken casserole left over from lunch any more. Actually I didn't really feel hungry then in any case.

So we got up from the table to go and play, but Alec's mum told us to be very good and not make a lot of mess in Alec's room, because she'd spent all morning tidying it up.

'We'll play trains and play with my little cars, and we can

play marbles and football!' said Alec.

'Oh no, you don't!' said Alec's mum. 'I don't want you turning your room into a shambles. Think of some nice quiet game to play.'

'Like what?' asked Alec.

'I know!' said Alec's dad. 'I'll teach you the most intellectually stimulating game in the world! You two go up to Alec's room and I'll be with you in a minute.'

So we went up to Alec's room, and his mum was right, it was ever so tidy, and then his dad came in with a box of chessmen under his arm.

'Chess?' said Alec. 'But we don't know how to play chess!'

'Well, I'm going to teach you,' said his dad. 'Just you wait – it's a wonderful game!'

And he was right, chess is really interesting. Alec's dad showed us how to put the chessmen out on the board, which is like a draughts board (I'm great at draughts!), and he told us which were the pawns and castles and bishops and knights, and the king and queen, and he showed us how to move them and capture the other player's pieces.

'It's like a battle between two armies,' said Alec's dad, 'with you two as the generals.'

Then Alec's dad picked up a pawn in each hand and closed his fists over them and asked me to choose. I got White and we started to play. Alec's dad, who is really fantastic, stayed to give advice and tell us when we did things wrong. Alec's mum came in, and she looked pleased to see us sitting at Alec's table playing chess. Then Alec's dad moved one of Alec's bishops for him and he laughed and said I'd lost.

'There,' said Alec's dad. 'I think you've got the idea now. So let Nicholas have Black for a change, and you can go on playing quietly by yourselves.'

And he went off with Alec's mum, telling her it was easy enough to handle children if you knew how, and was she sure there wasn't any chicken casserole left?

The only trouble with the black chessmen was that they were rather sticky from the jam on Alec's fingers, same as anything he touches.

'Join battle!' shouted Alec. 'Charge! Crash, bang!'

And he moved a pawn. Then I moved my knight, and the knight is the hardest one to move because first it goes straight ahead and then it goes sideways, but it's the most fun too because it can jump.

'Sir Lancelot fears no foe!' I shouted.

'Charge! Boom boom boom boom boom!' said Alec, pretending to be a drum and shoving several pawns forward with the back of his hand.

'Hey, you're not allowed to do that!' I said.

'Look to yourself, cowardly minion!' shouted Alec; you see, we'd both been watching this film on telly last Thursday, all about knights and old castles and that. So I pushed my pawns with both hands too, making a noise like a cannon and a machine gun, ratatatatat! And when my pawns collided with Alec's pawns lots of them fell over.

'Hold on!' said Alec. 'That doesn't count. You were being a machine gun, and they didn't have machine guns in the old days, just cannon, crash bang! Or swords going swoosh! It's no good playing chess if you're going to cheat!'

Alec had a point there, so I said all right. We went on playing chess; I moved my bishop, but it was rather tricky, because of all the pawns who'd fallen over on the board, and Alec flicked his finger like when you're playing marbles and he shot my bishop right against my knight, and my knight fell over. So then I did the same with my castle, and I hit his queen.

'That doesn't count!' said Alec. 'Castles go straight ahead, and you moved it sideways like a bishop.'

'Victory!' I shouted. 'Victory is ours! Charge, brave knights! Long live King Arthur! Crash! Bang!'

And I flicked no end of chessmen with my fingers. It was great!

'Wait a minute,' said Alec. 'It's too easy using our fingers. Let's use marbles for cannon balls. Crash bang!'

'OK,' I said, 'but there won't be room for them on the board.'

'I know!' said Alec. 'You go to one end of the room and I'll go to the other, and we can hide the chessmen behind the furniture legs.'

So Alec got his marbles out of his cupboard, which wasn't half as tidy as his room; lots of things fell out on the floor, and I picked up a black pawn and a white pawn and closed my fists over them and told Alec to choose, and he got White. We started shooting marbles at the chessmen, shouting, 'Crash bang!' and our chessmen were well hidden, so it was quite difficult to knock them over.

'Listen,' I said. 'Suppose we used the carriages of your train and some of your little cars to be tanks?'

So Alec got out his train and his little cars, and we put our soldiers in them, and off went the tanks, vroom vroom!

'The trouble is, we'll never knock the men over with our marbles if they're inside the tanks,' said Alec.

'Let's attack from the air,' I said.

So we filled our hands with marbles, and our hands were the planes, and we went 'vroom vroom!' And then, when the planes were passing over the tanks, we dropped the marbles, crash bang! But the marbles didn't hurt the carriages or the cars much, so Alec went to get his football, and he gave me another ball, a red and blue ball they bought him at the seaside, and we started kicking our balls at the tanks, and it was great! And then Alec kicked his ball a bit too hard, and it bounced off the door and landed on his desk and knocked over a bottle of ink, and Alec's mum came in.

Alec's mum was very cross. She told Alec he wouldn't be allowed a second helping of pudding at supper, and she told me it was getting late, and I should be getting home to my poor mother. And when I left there was still a lot of fuss going on at Alec's house, because his dad was telling him off now.

It's a shame we couldn't finish our game. I like chess, it's a great game! Next time it's fine we're going to play chess on the bit of waste ground. Vroom vroom crash bang!

Because the only trouble with chess is that it isn't really a good indoor game.

The Doctors

When I came into the school playground this morning Geoffrey came over to me, looking rather bothered. He said he'd heard some of the big boys say there were some doctors coming and we were going to have our chests X-rayed. And then the rest of the gang turned up.

'It's a lie!' said Rufus. 'The big boys are always telling lies.'

'What's a lie?' asked Jeremy.

'About the doctors coming this morning to give us injections,' said Rufus.

'You don't think it's true, do you?' asked Jeremy. He was really worried.

'Don't think what's true?' asked Max.

'About the doctors coming to do operations on us,' said Jeremy.

'I don't want them to!' shouted Max.

'Don't want them to do what?' asked Eddie.

'Take my appendicitis out!' said Max.

'What's an appendicitis?' asked Matthew.

'It's something they took out of me when I was little,' said Alec, 'so I don't care about those silly old doctors! They make me laugh!' And he laughed.

Then Old Spuds, one of the teachers, rang the bell and we

stood in line. We were all very bothered, except for Alec who was laughing like a drain and Cuthbert who hadn't heard about it because he was busy revising. When we got into the classroom our teacher said, 'Now, boys, this morning some doctors are coming to school to...'

But then she had to stop, because Cuthbert jumped up all of a sudden.

'Doctors?' shouted Cuthbert. 'I don't want to go and see any doctors! I won't go and see any doctors! I'm going to tell my mum on you! Anyway I can't go and see any doctors, I'm ill!'

Our teacher banged her desk with her ruler, and Cuthbert was still crying but she went on, 'There really isn't anything to worry about. You needn't act like babies! The doctors are simply coming to take X-ray pictures of your chests. It doesn't hurt at all, and...'

'Hey!' said Alec. 'They told me the doctors were coming to take our appendicitises out! I don't mind if it's appendicitises, but I'm not going to have any X-rays!'

'Appendicitises?' yelled Cuthbert, and he rolled about on the floor.

Our teacher was cross, and she banged the desk with her ruler again, she told Cuthbert to keep quiet if he didn't want her to give him nought out of ten for geography (we were having geography this lesson), and she said she'd have the next boy to speak expelled from school. So no one said anything except our teacher.

'Very well,' she said. 'An X-ray is simply a special kind of photograph which shows if your lungs are healthy. I'm sure you've had X-rays before, and you know what it's like, so there really is no point whatever in making a fuss.'

'Please, miss,' Matthew started, 'my lungs are…'

'Never mind your lungs! Come up to the blackboard and tell us what you know about the tributaries of the river Loire!' said our teacher.

Matthew had finished answering questions, and he'd only just gone to stand in the corner when Old Spuds came in.

'It's your class's turn now,' Old Spuds told our teacher.

'Right,' said our teacher. 'Everyone stand up, no talking, and get in line.'

'Even people standing in the corner?' asked Matthew.

But our teacher couldn't answer, because Cuthbert had started crying again, and shouting that he wasn't going to go, and if he'd been told beforehand he'd have brought a note from his parents excusing him, and he'd bring it tomorrow, and he held onto his desk with both hands and kicked like anything. So our teacher sighed and went up to him.

'Listen, Cuthbert,' said our teacher. 'I can assure you, there's no need to be frightened. The doctors won't even touch you! Why, it's great fun: they've come in a big lorry, and you can go up a flight of steps into the lorry, and it's very, very nice inside. Now listen to me: if you're good, I promise I'll ask you questions in the arithmetic lesson!'

'About fractions?' asked Cuthbert.

Our teacher said yes, so then Cuthbert let go of his desk and stood in line with the rest of us, trembling like a leaf and groaning the whole time.

When we got down into the playground, we met the big boys on their way back to their classroom.

'Does it hurt?' Geoffrey asked them.

'Ooh, it's awful!' said one of them. 'It burns and stings, it's

79

agony, and they go at you with great big knives and there's blood everywhere!'

And all the big boys went off, laughing like anything, and Cuthbert rolled on the ground and he was sick, and Old Spuds had to come and pick him up and take him to the sick room. Outside the school gate there was a big white lorry, with a little flight of steps for going up at the back, and another little flight of steps in the side of the lorry, near the front, for going down again. It was great. The Head was talking to a doctor in a white coat.

'That's the class I was telling you about,' said the Head.

'Don't you worry!' said the doctor. 'We're used to it! They'll toe the line with us; there won't be any trouble at all.'

And then we heard awful screaming. It was Old Spuds dragging Cuthbert by the arm.

'I think you'd better start with this boy,' said Old Spuds, 'he's rather highly strung.'

So one of the doctors picked Cuthbert up, and Cuthbert kicked him hard, screeching at him to let him go, and saying he'd been promised the doctors wouldn't touch him, and everyone was telling lies, and he was going to complain to the police. And then the doctor went into the lorry with Cuthbert, and we heard more yelling, and then a loud voice saying, 'Keep still! If you go on jiggling about like that I shall take you to hospital!' And then there was a lot of moaning and groaning, and we saw Cuthbert come out of the door at the side of the lorry, grinning all over his face, and he ran back into school.

'Right!' said one of the doctors, mopping his forehead. 'Come along, the first five boys, forward march!'

And as no one moved, the doctor pointed to five of us.

'You, you, you, you and you,' said the doctor.

'Why us and not him?' asked Geoffrey, pointing to Alec.

'Yes, why not him?' asked Rufus and Matthew and Max and me.

'The doctor said you, you, you, you and you,' said Alec. 'He didn't say me! So you have to go, and you and you and you and you. Not me!'

'Oh, do we? Well, if you're not going, he's not going and he's not going and he's not going and he's not going and I'm not going either!' said Geoffrey.

'When you've quite finished...!' said the doctor. 'Come along, you five, up you go! And get a move on!'

So we went up the steps. It was great inside the lorry! A doctor wrote our names down, and they told us to take off our shirts, they put us behind a piece of glass, one after another, and then they said that was all and to put our shirts on again.

'This lorry is fantastic!' said Rufus.

'See that little table?' asked Matthew.

'It must be fun, driving about in this,' I said.

'What's this thing? How does it work?' asked Max.

'Don't touch that!' shouted one of the doctors. 'Off you go! We're in a hurry. Go on, get moving...no! Not out the back! The other way!'

But Geoffrey, Matthew and Max had already started to go down the steps at the back, and we had a great time getting all mixed up with the rest of the gang coming up. And then the doctor standing by the door at the back stopped Rufus, who had gone all the way round and was trying to get back into the lorry, and said surely he'd been X-rayed already?

'No,' said Alec, 'it's me who's been X-rayed already.'

81

'And what's your name?' asked the doctor.

'Rufus,' said Alec.

'Some hope!' said Rufus.

'You there! Don't come up the steps at the front!' shouted one of the doctors.

And the doctors kept on taking X-rays, and lots of our gang kept going up and down the steps, and Alec was explaining to one of the doctors that it wasn't worth X-raying his chest

because he didn't have his appendicitis any more. Then the lorry driver leaned out and asked if he could drive off, because they were running very late.

'Yes, do that!' said one of the doctors in the lorry. 'They've all had their chests X-rayed now except for someone called Alec, who must be absent.'

So the lorry drove off, and the doctor who was standing on the pavement arguing with Alec turned round and shouted, 'Hey, hang on! Wait for me!' But the other doctors in the lorry didn't hear him, perhaps because we were all shouting so loud.

That doctor was furious, but it was a fair swap, really: they'd left us one of their doctors, but they still had one of our gang. Geoffrey had stayed behind in the lorry.

AMBULANCE

The New Bookshop

A new bookshop has just opened near our school, where the laundry used to be, and when lessons were over our gang went to take a look at it.

The shop window was great, all full of magazines and newspapers and books and pens, and we went in, and when the man in the bookshop saw us he gave us a big smile and said, 'Hullo, customers, I see! You must be from the school next door? I expect we'll soon be friends; my name is Mr Edwards.'

'I'm Nicholas,' I said.

'I'm Rufus,' Rufus said.

'I'm Geoffrey,' Geoffrey said.

'Do you have the latest number of *Socioeconomic Problems of the Western World?*' asked a man who had just come in.

'I'm Max,' said Max.

'Er, yes...pleased to meet you, sonny!' said Mr Edwards. 'I'll be with you in a moment, sir!' he told the man, and he started searching through a whole lot of magazines, and Alec asked, 'How much are those exercise books over there?'

'Hmph? What?' asked Mr Edwards. 'Oh, those! Fifty francs, young man.'

'We can get them at school for thirty francs,' said Alec.

Mr Edwards stopped looking for the magazine the man

wanted, and he turned round and said, 'Thirty francs? Exercise books with narrow feint and margin, a hundred pages?'

'Oh, no,' said Alec. 'The ones at school have fifty pages. Can I see that exercise book?'

'Yes,' said Mr Edwards, 'but wipe your hands. I see they're covered in butter from those sandwiches of yours.'

'Well, have you or have you not got the latest number of *Socioeconomic Problems of the Western World*?' asked the man.

'Yes, I'm sure I have, sir, I'll be able to lay my hand on it in just a minute,' said Mr Edwards. 'I've only just moved in, you see, I haven't got myself organized yet...here, what are you doing?'

Alec, who had gone behind the counter, told him, 'You were busy, so I went to take down the exercise book you say has a hundred pages in it myself, to have a look at it.'

'No! Don't touch! You'll bring the whole lot down!' shouted Mr Edwards. 'I was up all night arranging that display...here, that's the exercise book, and don't get any crumbs from that croissant of yours inside it!'

Then Mr Edwards picked up a magazine. 'Ah, here we are!' he said. '*Socioeconomic Problems of the Western World!*' But the man who wanted to buy the magazine had gone, so Mr Edwards sighed deeply, and put the magazine back.

'Hey, look!' said Rufus, planting his finger on one of the magazines. 'This one's the magazine my mum reads every week!'

'Good, good!' said Mr Edwards. 'Well, now your mother can come and buy her magazine here, can't she?'

'No,' said Rufus, 'my mum never buys it. Mrs Flowerdew next door gives Mum the magazine after she's read it herself. And Mrs Flowerdew doesn't buy the magazine either, she gets it by post every week.'

Mr Edwards looked at Rufus, without saying anything, and Geoffrey tugged my sleeve and said, 'Come and look at this!' And I went to look, and there were lots and lots of comic books on racks on the wall. It was great! First we looked at the covers, and then we tried turning them over to see inside, but the books wouldn't open properly because there were sort of clips holding them together, and we didn't like to take the clips off in case that annoyed Mr Edwards, and we didn't want to be a nuisance.

'I've got this one at home!' Geoffrey told me. 'It's a story all about airmen, vroom vroom! One of them is very brave, but there's always some baddies who want to sabotage his plane and make it crash; only when the plane does crash it's never the brave airman who's in it, it's one of his friends, so all his other friends think it was the airman who made the plane crash to get rid of his friend, but that isn't true, and then the airman finds out who really did it. Ever read it?'

'No,' I said, 'but I've read the one about

the cowboy and the deserted mine. Do you know that one? When he turns up and there are these masked men firing at him? Bang bang bang bang!'

'What is it now?' asked Mr Edwards, who was busy telling Matthew not to play about with the stand with books on it, the one that goes round and round so people can choose the book they want and then buy it.

'I'm telling him about a story I read,' I told Mr Edwards.

'Have you got it?' asked Geoffrey.

'What story is it?' asked Mr Edwards, running his fingers through his hair.

'It's all about this cowboy,' I said, 'and he comes to a deserted mine. And there are men waiting for him inside the mine, and…'

'I've read that one!' shouted Eddie. 'And the men start firing! Bang bang bang!'

'Bang! And then the sheriff says, "Howdy, pardner! We don't talk to strangers around these parts…"'

'That's right,' said Eddie, 'and then the cowboy draws his revolver and goes bang bang bang!'

'That will be quite enough of that!' said Mr Edwards.

'I like my story about the airman better,' said Geoffrey. 'Vroom vroom crash!'

'You and your soppy old airman!' I said. 'My cowboy story is much better than your airman story!'

'Oh, it is, is it?' said Geoffrey. 'Well, your cowboy story is the soppiest of the lot, so there!'

'Want me to punch your nose?' asked Eddie.

'Boys, boys!' shouted Mr Edwards.

And then we heard ever such a loud noise, and the whole

stand that goes round and round with the books on it had fallen over.

'I hardly even touched it!' shouted Matthew, very red in the face.

Mr Edwards wasn't looking at all pleased, and he said, 'That will do! Don't touch anything else! Do you or do you not want to buy something?'

'Ninety-nine, one hundred!' said Alec. 'No, there isn't any catch in it, that exercise book really does have a hundred pages. It's great! I'd like to buy it.'

Mr Edwards took the exercise book away from Alec, which was easy enough because Alec's hands are always slippery with butter; he looked inside the exercise book and he said, 'You little horror! You've left dirty finger-marks all over the pages! Oh, well, that's just too bad! That'll be fifty francs.'

'I know,' said Alec, 'but I haven't got any money. I'll ask my dad if he'll give me some when I go home for lunch, but I wouldn't count on it if I was you, because I was playing Dad up a bit yesterday and he said he saw he'd have to take quite a firm line with me.'

And it was getting quite late, so we all left, shouting, 'See you soon, Mr Edwards!'

Mr Edwards didn't even say goodbye; he was busy looking at the exercise book that Alec might be going to buy.

I'm really pleased we've got this new bookshop near school, and I know Mr Edwards will be glad to see us any time. Like Mum says, it's always a good thing to be on friendly terms with people in the shops because then they remember your face and you get good service.

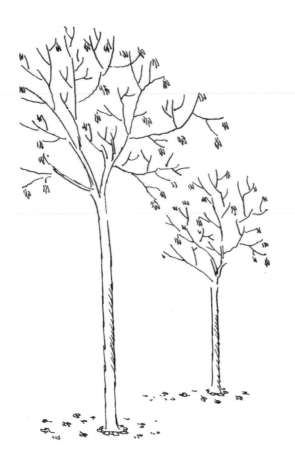

Rufus is Ill

We were in our classroom, doing arithmetic; it was a very hard sum about a farmer selling lots of eggs and apples, and Rufus put his hand up.

'Yes, Rufus?' asked our teacher.

'Please can I leave the room?' said Rufus. 'I'm not feeling well.'

Our teacher told Rufus to come up to her desk; she looked at him, she put her hand on his forehead and she said, 'No, you really don't look at all well. Run along to the sick room and tell them to see to you.'

So Rufus went off, looking very pleased, without finishing the sum. Then Matthew put his hand up, and our teacher told him to write out fifty times, 'I must not pretend to be ill so as to try to get out of finishing my sum.'

We saw Rufus out in the playground at break, and we went over to him.

'Did you go to the sick room?' I asked.

'No fear!' said Rufus. 'I hid till it was time for break.'

'Why didn't you go to the sick room?' asked Eddie.

'I'm not nuts!' said Rufus. 'Last time I went to the sick room they put iodine on my knee and it stung like mad.'

Then Geoffrey asked Rufus if he really felt ill, and Rufus asked him if he wanted to be thumped, and that made Matthew laugh a lot, and I don't remember too well just what the rest of the gang said and did, but pretty soon we were having a tremendous punch-up. Rufus was sitting in the middle of us, watching and shouting, 'Go on, hit him! Go on!'

As usual, Alec and Cuthbert weren't fighting. Cuthbert wasn't fighting because he was doing revision and because we're not allowed to thump him because of his glasses, and Alec wasn't fighting because he had two sandwiches to get finished before the end of break.

And then Mr Miller came running up. Mr Miller is a new teacher who isn't all that old, and he was on playground duty, helping Old Spuds, which is fair enough, because however good we are, doing playground duty must be quite hard work.

'Well, what's up now, you little barbarians?' asked Mr Miller. 'It's detention for the lot of you!'

'Not me!' said Rufus. 'I'm ill.'

'Huh!' said Geoffrey.

'Want me to thump you?' asked Rufus.

'Silence!' shouted Mr Miller. 'Silence, or I can assure you you'll all be feeling ill!'

So we shut up, and Mr Miller told Rufus to come over there.

'What's the matter with you?' asked Mr Miller.

Rufus said he didn't feel well.

'Did you tell your parents?' asked Mr Miller.

'Yes,' said Rufus, 'I told my mum this morning.'

'In that case,' said Mr Miller, 'why did your mother let you come to school?'

'Well,' Rufus explained, 'I tell my mum I don't feel well every morning, so she wasn't to know, was she? But this time I really and truly don't feel very well.'

Mr Miller looked at Rufus and scratched his head and told him he'd have to go to the sick room.

'No,' shouted Rufus.

'What do you mean, no?' asked Mr Miller. 'If you're not well you must go to the sick room! And when I tell you to do something you have to obey me!'

So then Mr Miller took hold of Rufus's arm, but Rufus started shouting, 'No, no! I won't go! I won't go!' and he rolled about on the ground crying.

'Don't you hit him!' said Alec, who had just finished his sandwiches. 'Can't you see he isn't feeling well?'

Mr Miller's jaw dropped and he looked at Alec.

'But I wasn't going to...' he started, and then he went bright red and he shouted at Alec to mind his own business, and he gave him detention.

'Oh, honestly!' Alec shouted back. 'You mean you're giving me detention just because that silly twit is ill?'

'Want me to thump you?' asked Rufus, who had stopped crying.

'Huh!' said Geoffrey.

And we all started shouting and arguing, and Rufus sat down to watch us, and Old Spuds came running up too.

'Having trouble, Mr Miller?' asked Old Spuds.

'It's because of Rufus feeling ill,' said Eddie.

'I didn't ask you, Eddie,' said Old Spuds. 'Mr Miller, kindly give that pupil detention.'

And Mr Miller gave Eddie detention. Alec was pleased, because if you get detention it's more fun to have company.

Then Mr Miller told Old Spuds about Rufus not wanting to go to the sick room, and Alec actually daring to tell him not to hit Rufus when he'd never dreamt of hitting Rufus, and how we were totally, utterly, absolutely, impossible! That's what he said, and when he got to impossible his voice sounded like my mum's when I've really gone and upset her badly.

Old Spuds stroked his chin, and then he took hold of Mr Miller's arm; he walked a little way off with him, he put a hand on his shoulder and he talked to him for a long time, in a low voice. And then Old Spuds and Mr Miller came back to us.

'Now, let me show you how to handle them!' said Old Spuds, grinning all over his face.

And he beckoned Rufus over to him.

'You will oblige me by coming to the sick room with me, and no more nonsense, right?'

'No!' shouted Rufus. And he rolled around on the ground crying and shouting. 'Won't! Won't! Won't!'

'You mustn't use force on him,' said Jeremy.

It was really great after that! Old Spuds went bright red, he gave Jeremy detention, and then he gave Max detention for laughing. What surprised me was that Mr Miller was grinning all over his face now.

And then Old Spuds told Rufus, 'Off you go to the sick room this instant! No more arguing!'

So Rufus saw this wasn't the time for acting up any more and he said oh, all right, he'd go so long as they didn't put any iodine on his knees.

'Iodine?' said Old Spuds. 'No one's going to put any iodine on you! But once you're better I want you to come and see me. We have a little account to settle! Now, off you go with Mr Miller.'

And we all started off for the sick room, with Old Spuds shouting, 'No, no, not all of you! Just Rufus! The sick room is not a playground. And your friend may be infectious!'

We all thought that was very funny, except for Cuthbert, who's dead scared of catching things from other people.

And after that Old Spuds rang the bell, and we went back to our classroom while Mr Miller took Rufus home. Rufus was in luck; it was grammar next lesson.

And luckily it wasn't a very serious illness.

Measles, that's what Rufus and Mr Miller have got.

Athletics

I don't know if I told you before, but there's this piece of waste ground where our gang sometimes plays.

That waste ground is fantastic! There's grass there, and stones, an old mattress, a car which doesn't have any wheels but it's still terrific and it can be a plane, vroom vroom! Or a bus, ding ding! And there are tin cans and sometimes cats too, but you can't play with the cats much because when they see us coming they go away.

We were on the waste ground, all our gang, wondering what to play, because Alec's football has been confiscated until the end of term.

'Let's play war games,' said Rufus.

'You know whenever we play war games we fight because no one wants to be the enemy,' said Eddie.

'I've got an idea!' said Matthew. 'Let's have an athletics meeting!'

And Matthew told us he'd seen one of them on the telly, and it was great. There were no end of different sports, with every-one doing lots of different events at the same time, and the winners climbed up on a platform and people gave them medals.

'So where are you going to get a platform and some medals?' asked Jeremy.

'We can pretend they're there,' said Matthew.

That sounded a good idea, so we said OK.

'Right!' said Matthew. 'First we'll do the high jump.'

'I'm not doing the high jump,' said Alec.

'You'll have to do the high jump,' said Matthew. 'Everyone has to do the high jump!'

'Oh no, they don't,' said Alec. 'I'm in the middle of eating my sandwiches, and if I do the high jump I'll be sick, and if I'm sick I won't be able to finish my sandwiches before supper, so I'm not doing the high jump.'

'Oh, all right,' said Matthew. 'You can hold the string for us to jump over. We need a piece of string.'

So we searched our pockets and we found marbles, buttons, stamps and a toffee, but no string.

'We'd better use someone's belt,' said Geoffrey.

'Don't be daft,' said Rufus. 'You can't do the high jump if you have to hold your trousers up at the same time.'

'Alec isn't going to do the high jump,' said Eddie, 'so he can lend us his belt.'

'I'm not wearing a belt,' said Alec. 'My trousers keep up by themselves.'

'I'll see if I can find a bit of string lying around somewhere,' said Jeremy.

Max said it was a fat lot of use looking for a bit of string in the middle of the waste ground, and there wasn't much point spending the afternoon looking for a bit of string, and why not do something else?

'Hey, I know!' shouted Geoffrey. 'Let's have a competition to see who can walk on his hands longest. Look at me! Look at me!'

And Geoffrey started walking on his hands. He's very good at walking on his hands, but Matthew told him he'd never seen a walking-on-your-hands event in any athletics meeting, silly twit!

'Silly twit? Who's a silly twit?' said Geoffrey, and he stopped walking on his hands; he stood the right way up and went over to thump Matthew.

'Listen, everyone,' said Rufus, 'it's not worth coming to the waste ground just to fight and fool about! We can do that any day at school!'

Rufus was right, so Matthew and Geoffrey stopped fighting, and Geoffrey told Matthew he'd take him on where he wanted, when he wanted, and any way he wanted.

'You sure do scare the living daylights out of me, kid!' said Matthew. 'Back home on the range we know how to deal with coyotes like you!'

'Look, are you playing cowboys or are you doing the high jump?' asked Alec.

'Ever see anyone do the high jump without something to jump over?' asked Max.

'Sure thing, kid!' said Geoffrey. 'But I'm mighty quick on the draw!'

And Geoffrey went 'bang bang!', using his finger for a gun, and Rufus clutched his tummy with both hands and said, 'Got me, Butch!' and he fell down in the grass.

'If we can't do the high jump,' said Matthew, 'we can run races.'

'If we had some string,' said Max, 'we could have a hurdle race.'

Matthew said that we didn't have any string, so we'd have a hundred metres race from the fence to the old car.

'Is that a hundred metres?' asked Eddie.

'What does it matter?' asked Matthew. 'First to reach the car has won the hundred metres, so too bad for the others!'

But Max said it wouldn't be a real hundred metres race, because in real races there's a string at the end so the winner can breast the tape. And Matthew told Max he was getting on his nerves, him and his string, and Max told him it's no good organizing an athletics meeting if you don't have any string, and Matthew said he might not have any string but he had a good hard hand, and he was going to smack Matthew's face with it. And Max said just let him try it, and Matthew would have tried it too, only Max kicked him first.

When they'd finished their fight Matthew was very cross. He said we didn't know the first thing about athletics meetings, and we were a soppy lot, and then we saw Jeremy come running up, very pleased with himself.

'Hey, look at this! I found a bit of wire!'

So Matthew said that was great, we could carry on with the athletics meeting now, and since we'd all of us had about enough of doing the high jump and sprinting, we'd throw the hammer. Matthew explained that the hammer wasn't a real hammer, it was a weight tied to a piece of string and you made it go round and round very fast and then let go, and whoever threw the hammer farthest was the winner. Matthew made the hammer out of a stone with one end of the wire wound round it.

'I'll have first go, because it was my idea,' said Matthew. 'You just watch me throw it!'

Matthew turned round and round on the spot lots of times, swinging the hammer about, and then he let it go.

We stopped the athletics meeting, and Matthew said he was the winner. But the others said no he wasn't, they hadn't had a go at throwing the hammer, so we couldn't know who'd won.

But I think Matthew was right, he'd have won anyway. It was a really tremendous throw, all the way from the waste ground right into Mr Compani the grocer's shop window!

The Secret Code

Have you ever noticed how difficult it is when you want to talk to your friends in class, and people keep on interrupting you? Of course you can talk to the person sitting next to you all right, but however quietly you try to talk your teacher seems to hear you, and she says, 'If you like the sound of your own voice so much you can come up to the blackboard and answer questions, and then we'll see if you still have such a lot to say!' And she asks you all the administrative departments of France and their capital cities, and there's trouble. Well, you can always pass round a note with whatever you want to say written on it, but somehow your teacher nearly always sees the note being passed, and you have to take it up to her desk, and then you have to take it to the Head, and since it says 'Rufus is a twit, pass it on!' or 'Eddie has a face like a monkey, pass it on!' the Head tells you that at this rate you'll end up an illiterate jailbird, which will cause your poor parents great distress, when they're making such sacrifices to provide you with a good education. And he gives you detention.

That's why we liked the idea Geoffrey told us at break today.

'I've invented a secret code. It's great!' Geoffrey said. 'Our gang are the only ones who'll be able to understand it.'

And he showed us. You made a different gesture for each

letter; for instance, putting your finger on your nose was 'a', putting your finger on your left eye was 'b', putting your finger on your right eye was 'c'. There were different things for all the letters, like scratching your ear, or rubbing your chin or tapping your head, all the way through to the letter 'z', which was squinting. It was great!

Matthew wasn't too happy about it; he said the alphabet was a secret code to him anyway, and he'd rather wait till break to tell the gang what he wanted to say instead of learning how to spell so as to talk to us. And of course Cuthbert wasn't interested in the secret code. He's top of the class and teacher's pet, so he'd rather listen to our teacher and get asked questions in lessons. Cuthbert is nuts!

But the rest of us thought the code was a good idea. Secret codes are very useful, anyway; when you're fighting your enemies you can say all sorts of things to each other and they don't understand and then you win!

So we asked Geoffrey to teach us his code. We all stood round him and he told us to copy him: he touched his nose with his finger and we touched our noses with our own fingers; he touched his eyes and we all touched our own eyes. We'd just got to squinting when Mr Miller came along. Mr Miller is a new teacher who's a bit older than the big boys, but

not that much older, and I think it's the first time he's had a job in a school.

'Listen,' Mr Miller told us, 'I'm not going to be fool enough to ask you what you think you're up to, making faces like that, all I'm saying is that if you carry on with it I'm giving you all detention, understand?'

And he went away.

'Right,' said Geoffrey, 'Now, do you all remember the code?'

'The bit that bothers me,' said Jeremy, 'is touching your right knee and your left knee for "i" and "o". I keep getting right and left mixed up, like Mum when she's driving Dad's car.'

'Oh, that doesn't matter,' said Geoffrey.

'What do you mean, it doesn't matter?' said Jeremy. 'Suppose I want to call you an idiot and call you an odoit, it's not the same, is it?'

'Who are you calling an idiot, idiot?' asked Geoffrey.

But they didn't have time to fight, because Mr Miller rang the bell for the end of break. Break is getting shorter and shorter all the time, now Mr Miller's on playground duty.

We stood in line, and Geoffrey told us, 'I'm going to give you a message in class, and at next break we'll see how many people got it. I warn you, everyone in our gang has to know the secret code!'

'Oh, great!' said Matthew. 'So Geoffrey's decided that if I don't know his silly old code I can't be in the gang any more! Oh, that's marvellous!'

So then Mr Miller told Matthew, 'You will write out fifty times, "I must not talk while standing in line, especially when I have the whole of break to make half-witted comments to my friends."'

'If you'd used the secret code you wouldn't have got those lines,' said Alec, and Mr Miller gave him the same lines to write out too. Alec is always good for a laugh!

In class our teacher told us to get out our exercise books and copy down the sums she was going to write on the board for us to do at home. That was a nuisance, specially because when Dad gets home from the office he's tired, and he isn't keen on doing arithmetic homework. And then, while our teacher was writing on the board, we all turned round to look at Geoffrey, waiting for him to begin his message. So then Geoffrey started making gestures, and it wasn't all that easy to understand, because he went rather fast, and then he stopped to write in his exercise book, and then, when we were looking, he started making gestures again, and he looked awfully funny sticking his fingers in his ears and tapping himself on the head.

Geoffrey's message was ever so long, which meant we couldn't copy down the sums. We were afraid of missing some of the letters and not understanding the message, so of course we had to keep on looking at Geoffrey, and Geoffrey sits in the back row.

And then Geoffrey rubbed his right foot for 't' and put his

tongue out for 'h', and his jaw dropped, he stopped, we all turned round again and we saw that our teacher had stopped writing on the board and was watching Geoffrey.

'Yes, Geoffrey,' said our teacher. 'Like your friends, I am fascinated by your curious antics. But don't you think this has gone on long enough? Go and stand in the corner, you will not go out at break, and by tomorrow you will write out one hundred times, "I must not act the fool in class and be a bad influence on my friends, preventing them from working."'

We hadn't got the gist of the message at all. So we waited for Geoffrey coming out of school, and when he came out we could see he was very annoyed.

'What were you saying to us in class?' I asked.

'Leave me alone!' shouted Geoffrey. 'Anyway, I'm not using the secret code any more, and I'm never going to speak to you again, so there!'

It wasn't till next day Geoffrey told us what his message was. He'd been saying:

'Stop staring at me like that, you lot, or our teacher will notice something.'

Mary Jane's Birthday

Today I was invited to Mary Jane's birthday party. Mary Jane may be a girl, but she's all right: she has yellow hair and blue eyes and pink cheeks, and she's the daughter of Mr and Mrs Campbell who live next door. Mr Campbell is in charge of the shoe departments of the Save-It chain stores, and Mrs Campbell plays the piano, and she's always singing the same song, which has loud bits in it, and we can hear them ever so well in our house every evening.

Mum had bought Mary Jane a present: a toy kitchen with pots and pans, and I didn't see how anyone could really have any fun with a toy like that. And Mum had made me put on my sailor suit with the tie, and she'd brushed my hair and put brilliantine on it, and she said I must be very good and act like a little gentleman, and she went over to Mary Jane's house with me. I was pleased because I like birthday parties and I like Mary Jane. Of course, when you go to a birthday party there isn't always such a great gang as Alec and Geoffrey and Eddie and Rufus and Matthew and Jeremy and Max, who are my gang at school, but you're bound to have a good time. There's birthday cake, and you can play cowboys and cops and robbers, and it's great!

Mary Jane's mum opened the door, and she gave a little

squeal as if she was surprised to see me, but she was the one who rang up Mum to invite me! She was very nice, she said I was a good boy, and she called Mary Jane to come and see the lovely present I'd brought. And Mary Jane came in, looking all pink, in a white frock with lots of little frills; it was really great. I felt a bit silly giving her the present, because I was sure she wouldn't think much of it, and I quite agreed with Mrs Campbell when she told Mum oh, we really shouldn't have! But Mary Jane seemed very pleased with the toy kitchen. Girls are funny! Then Mum left, telling me again to be very good.

I went into Mary Jane's house, and there were two more girls wearing frocks with lots of little frills. They were called Melanie and Eve, and Mary Jane told me they were her two best friends. We shook hands and I went and sat down in an armchair in a corner, while Mary Jane showed her best friends the toy kitchen and Melanie said she'd got one just the same, only better, but Eve said she was sure Melanie's toy kitchen wasn't half as good as the dolls' dinner service Eve got for her birthday. And they all three started arguing.

Then the doorbell rang several times, and lots of little girls came in, all wearing dresses with frills on and bringing silly presents, and one or two of them had brought their dolls with them. If I'd known I'd have brought my football. Then Mrs Campbell said, 'Well, I think everyone's here, so let's go into the dining room and have tea.'

When I realized I was the only boy there I wanted to go back home, but I didn't dare, and I

felt very hot in the face when we went into the dining room.
Mrs Campbell made me sit in between Lisa and Barbara, and
Mary Jane told me they were her two best friends too.

Mrs Campbell gave us paper hats to put on. Mine was a
pointed clown's hat with elastic under the chin. All the girls
laughed when they looked at me, and my face felt hotter than
ever, and my tie seemed very tight.

Tea wasn't bad: there were little biscuits, and hot chocolate
to drink, and they had a cake with candles on it and Mary Jane
blew them out, and everybody clapped. It was funny, though,
I didn't feel very hungry myself, and apart from breakfast and
lunch and supper, tea is the meal I like best, almost as much as
the sandwich I take to school for break.

The girls ate a lot, and they kept talking all at once and
giggling and pretending to give their dolls pieces of cake to eat.

Then Mrs Campbell said we'd go back into the sitting room,
and I went and sat down in the armchair in the corner again.

After that Mary Jane stood in the middle of the room with
her hands behind her back, and she recited something or other
about little birds. When she'd finished we all clapped and Mrs
Campbell asked if anyone else would like to do something,
like reciting or dancing or singing?

'How about Nicholas?' asked Mrs Campbell. 'I'm sure a
good little boy like Nicholas knows a poem to recite!'

I had a huge lump in my throat and I shook my head, and
they all laughed. With or without my pointed hat, I must have
looked a right Charlie! Then Barbara gave Janet her doll to
look after, and she sat down to play a piece on the piano, with
her tongue sticking out, but she forgot the end of it and she
started to cry. Then Mrs Campbell got up and said that was

lovely, and she hugged Barbara and asked us all to clap, and the girls all clapped.

Then Mary Jane put her presents in the middle of the floor, and the girls started squealing and giggling like mad, but there wasn't one decent toy among the lot: there was my kitchen, another, bigger toy kitchen, a toy sewing machine, dolls' dresses, a little cupboard and a toy iron.

'Why not play with your little friends?' Mrs Campbell asked me.

I looked at her and I didn't say anything. Then Mrs Campbell clapped her hands and she cried, 'I know! We'll dance! I'll play the piano and you can all dance!'

I didn't want to, but Mrs Campbell took my arm, I had to hold hands with Bella and Eve, and we all got into a circle, and while Mrs Campbell played her song on the piano we started dancing round. I was thinking that if the gang could see me now I'd have to leave school and go to a new one.

And then the doorbell rang, and it was Mum coming to fetch me. I was ever so pleased to see her.

'Nicholas is such a dear!' Mrs Campbell told Mum. 'I've never known such a good little boy. A little shy, perhaps, but he's certainly the best-behaved of all my little guests!'

Mum looked pleased, but rather surprised. When I got home I sat down in an armchair and I didn't say anything, and when Dad got in he looked at me and he asked Mum what was up.

'I'm very proud of him, that's what!' said Mum. 'He went to Mary Jane's birthday party, he was the only boy there, and Mrs Campbell told me he behaved better than anyone else.'

Dad rubbed his chin, he patted me on the head, he wiped the brilliantine off his hand with his handkerchief and he asked if I'd had a nice time. So then I started to cry.

Dad laughed, and this evening he took me out to see a film all about cowboys knocking each other out and shooting their guns!

René Goscinny

René Goscinny is the world-famous writer and creator, along with Albert Uderzo, of the adventures of Asterix the Gaul. Born in Paris in 1926, Goscinny lived in Buenos Aires and New York. He returned to France in the 1950s where he met Jean-Jacques Sempé and they collaborated on picture strips and then stories about Nicholas, the popular French schoolboy. An internationally successful children's author, who also won awards for his animated cartoons, Goscinny died in 1977.

Jean-Jacques Sempé

Jean-Jacques Sempé is one of the most famous cartoonists and illustrators in the world and his work is featured in countless magazines and newspapers. Born in Bordeaux, France in 1932, Sempé was expelled from school for bad behaviour. He enjoyed a variety of jobs, from travelling toothpaste salesman to soldier, before winning an art prize in 1952. Although Sempé was never trained formally as an artist, more than twenty volumes of his drawings have been published, in thirty countries. He lives in Paris.

Anthea Bell

Anthea Bell was awarded the Independent Foreign Fiction Prize and the Helen and Kurt Wolff Prize (USA) in 2002 for her translation of W.G. Sebald's Austerlitz. *Her many works of translation from French and German (for which she has received several other awards) include the* Nicholas *books and, with Derek Hockridge, the entire* Asterix the Gaul *saga by René Goscinny and Albert Uderzo.*

Have you read...

Nicholas

Whether at home or at school, Nicholas is forever in some
kind of trouble. In this first book in the *Nicholas* series, he
becomes involved with a shiny red bike, a new boy at school
and a dog called Rex.

Nicholas Again

In this collection of adventures, Nicholas and his friends go fishing for tadpoles, visit an art gallery and play a complicated game of football, but, of course, things don't quite go according to plan.

Nicholas on Holiday

The stories in this book all take place during the long summer holidays. Nicholas meets a new gang of friends at the seaside, and they always find ways of amusing themselves, even when it's raining outside.

Nicholas in Trouble

Things are never easy for Nicholas and his friends. The lady in the sweet shop won't let them buy chocolate, their teacher won't let them play Geoffrey's fantastic new game and Jeremy is none too pleased about his new little brother.

To find out more about Nicholas and his friends or to sign up to join the Nicholas Club, visit www.phaidon.com/nicholas